The Town Mouse and the Country Mouse

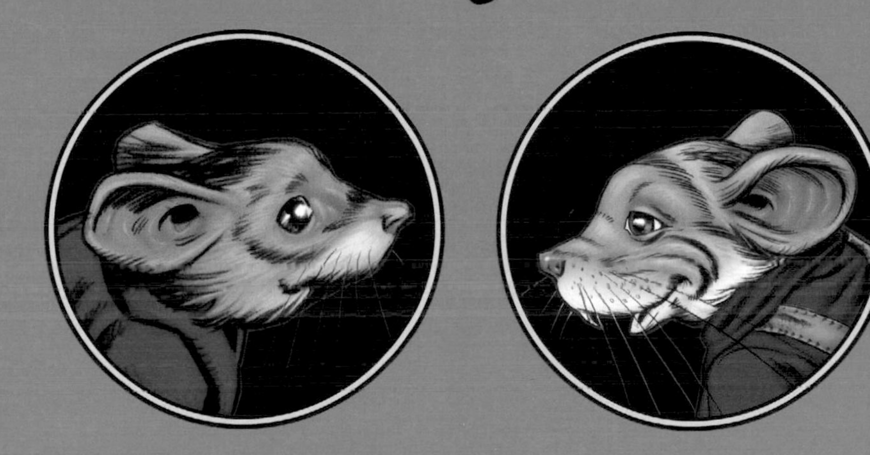

Adapted by Christopher E. Long
Illustrated by Mark Bloodworth

First published in 2013 by Wayland

Wayland
338 Euston Road
London NW1 3BH

Wayland Australia
Level 17/207 Kent Street
Sydney, NSW 2000

Adapted Text by Christopher E. Long
Illustrations by Mark Bloodworth
Colours by Hi-Fi
Edited by Stephanie Hedlund and Rochelle Baltzer
Interior Layout by Kristen Fitzner Denton and Alyssa Peacock
Book Design and Packaging by Shannon Eric Denton
Cover Design by Alyssa Peacock

A cataloguing record for this title is available at the British Library.
Dewey number: 398.2'452-dc23

Printed in China

ISBN: 978 0 7502 7785 3

Wayland is a division of Hachette Children's Books, an Hachette UK company.
www.hachette.co.uk

One day, Town Mouse went to visit his cousin.

Country Mouse welcomed Town Mouse into his home.

'Your home is small' Town Mouse said.

'But it's warm and peaceful' Country Mouse said.

Country Mouse served Town Mouse dinner.

EARL GREY

'Everything is much better in town'
Town Mouse said.

'Come with me and I'll show you how to live' Town Mouse said.

'Your home is very large' Country Mouse said.

'Are you hungry, cousin?'
Town Mouse asked.

'Yes, I am' said Country Mouse.

'This is what we eat in town'
Town Mouse said.

Suddenly, the cousins heard barking.

They had to run and hide.

Once the dogs had left, Country Mouse said goodbye to Town Mouse.

'Better beans and bacon in peace than cakes in fear' he said.

The moral of the story is:

Better a little in safety, than much surrounded by danger.

SHORT TALES
Fairy Tales

Titles in the Short Tales Fairy Tales series:

Aladdin and the Lamp

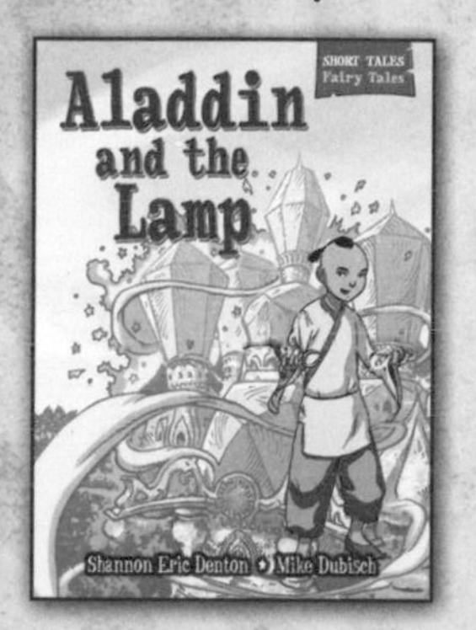

978 0 7502 7750 1

Beauty and the Beast

978 0 7502 7752 5

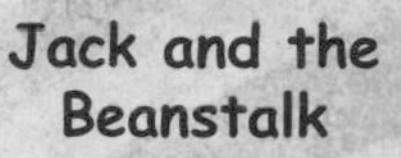

978 0 7502 7751 8

Puss in Boots

978 0 7502 7754 9

Sleeping Beauty

978 0 7502 7755 6

The Little Mermaid

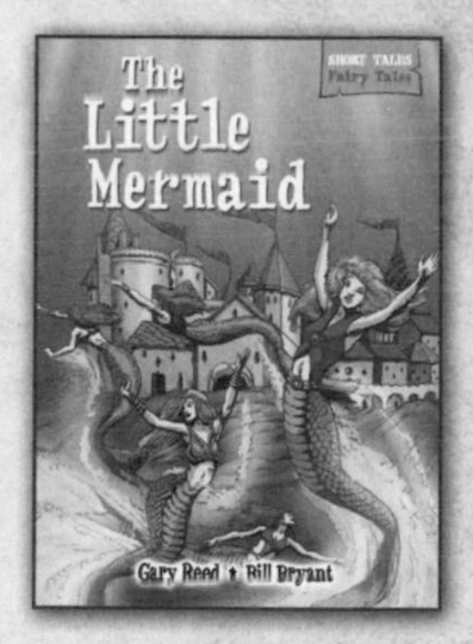

978 0 7502 7753 2

WAYLAND

www.waylandbooks.co.uk

Follow us on Twitter @waylandbooks | Find us on Facebook Wayland Books

SHORT TALES
Fables

Titles in the Short Tales Fables series:

The Ants and the Grasshopper

978 0 7502 7756 3

The Boy Who Cried Wolf

978 0 7502 7757 0

The Fox and the Grapes

978 0 7502 7758 7

The Lion and the Mouse

978 0 7502 7783 9

The Tortoise and the Hare

978 0 7502 7784 6

The Town Mouse and the Country Mouse

978 0 7502 7785 3

WAYLAND

www.waylandbooks.co.uk

Follow us on Twitter @waylandbooks | Find us on Facebook Wayland Books